Ceep

For my Uncle Lalo, a grand storyteller, and
for my friend Arturo Madrid, who
loves New Mexico. PM

For Meilia, Sabrina, Madeline, Kenneth,
Ira, Kyle, Arden, and James. ALC

Text copyright © 2008 by Pat Mora
Illustrations copyright © 2008 by Amelia Lau Carling
Published in Canada and the USA in 2008 by Groundwood Books
First paperback edition 2011

Groundwood Books / House of Anansi Press
110 Spadina Avenue, Suite 801, Toronto, Ontario M5V 2K4
or c/o Publishers Group West
1700 Fourth Street, Berkeley, CA 94710

We acknowledge for their financial support of our publishing
program the Government of Canada through the
Canada Book Fund (CBF).

Library and Archives Canada Cataloguing in Publication
Mora, Pat
Abuelos / story by Pat Mora ; pictures by Amelia Lau Carling.
ISBN 978-1-55498-101-4
I. Carling, Amelia Lau II. Title.
PZ8.1.M668Ab 2011   j813'.54   C2010-904469-X

The illustrations were done in watercolor with pastels and colored pencils.
Design by Michael Solomon

Abuelos

STORY BY

Pat Mora

PICTURES BY

Amelia Lau Carling

GROUNDWOOD BOOKS
HOUSE OF ANANSI PRESS
TORONTO BERKELEY

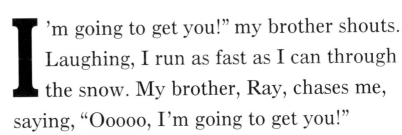

I'm going to get you!" my brother shouts. Laughing, I run as fast as I can through the snow. My brother, Ray, chases me, saying, "Ooooo, I'm going to get you!"

I run into the house my father built. He grew up in this little pueblo, and now we have moved back here to live. My parents teach at the school.

"Qué frío!" Papá says, coming in after me. "Help me build a good fire, Amelia." He rubs his cold hands together and then rubs my hands in his. "So, what do you think of your first winter in these New Mexico mountains?"

"It's cold," I say, helping my mother set the table.

After supper I stretch out in front of the fire by Grandpa and read my book. The fire crackles and pops. Outside, the wind howls.

"Chocolate?" Papá says, offering us cups of hot, foamy chocolate with cinnamon.

"Oooooo," my brother squeals in a high voice, trying to scare me. "Oooooo, the old mountain men are coming to visit Amelia."

I move closer to my father.

"Tell her, Papá," says Ray. "Tell her again about the men who are going to come down from the mountains."

My father pats my head softly. "When your grandfather was a little boy here, Amelia, on a windy December night like this, the old men of the mountains – los abuelos – would come down to make sure that the children had all been good."

"But abuelos means grandfathers, right?" I ask.

"Yes," says Papá, "but once abuelos was also used for the old mountain men."

"I'm scared," I say. "Why do they have to come now?"

"Don't worry, Amelia," says Grandpa. "Remember that when the abuelos come, there will be a dance at your aunt's house. Everyone in the pueblo will bring good things to eat. The night the abuelos come, the whole town joins the party."

"But be good now, both of you," says Mamá. "Don't play near the river, and don't go out alone at night. The old mountain men come down to make sure that children are minding their parents."

"Really, Papá?" I ask. "Are you teasing us? Do they really come down?"

"They say the abuelos sleep high in the mountains in dark, smoky caves," Papá says. "Once a year, the sooty, hairy abuelos come down to make sure all the children are behaving."

Ray whispers, "Da-a-a-ark," right in my ear.

"Stop it, Ray," I say. "Don't scare me!"

"Ya, ya, ya," Mamá says. "That's enough, Raymundo."

My father grins and gives me one of his big bear hugs. "No one is going to hurt you, Amelia," he says. "You know how Halloween is scary and fun? So is the coming of the abuelos."

After Mamá tucks us in, I look out the window and wonder if the abuelos are asleep in their caves.

"Amel-l-lia," my brother sings in a spooky voice. "They're com-m-m-ing."

"Mamá!" I call.

I hear the wind outside. I listen. I think I hear the abuelos snoring and snoring. What if they chase me? What if they chase Ray? I hide under the covers.

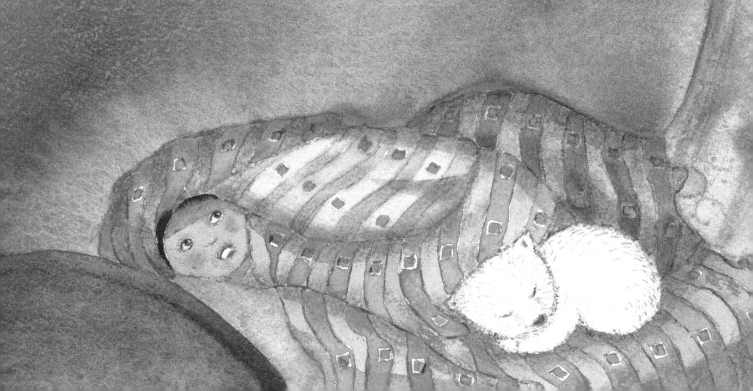

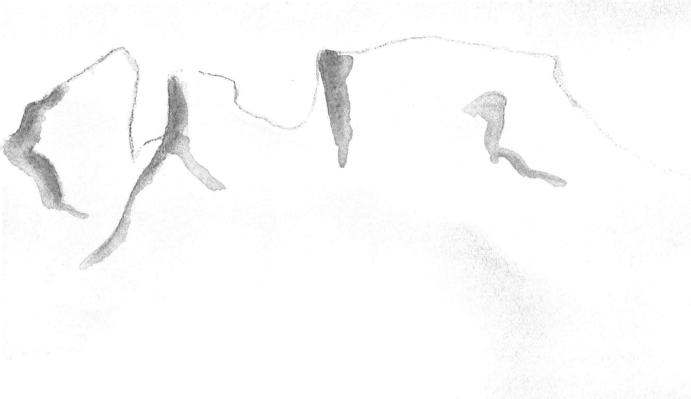

The next day, when I am gathering wood for the fire, Ray calls, "Oooooo, here I come."

Ray looks silly in Grandpa's old clothes. When he chases me, I drop the wood and start to run. I fall in the snow. I pull myself up and run faster. Ray catches my coat and won't let go.

"I'm a hairy, sooty abuelo," he whines. "Have you been goo-oo-ood?"

"Yes," I say, laughing and trying to pull away.

I yank hard and run into the house. It smells like apples.

"Wash your hands and set the table, por favor, Amelia," Mamá says, giving me a hug.

"Sí, Mamá," I say. I mind her right away in case the abuelos are listening. She has made lots of empanadas. I smell the little apple turnovers.

"Later, Amelia," Mamá says. "We'll have them later."

Ray comes in and tries to scare us.

"You'd better behave yourself, Raymundo," Mamá says. "The abuelos chase boys who don't behave, remember? Clean up for dinner now."

Then Papá comes in. "It sure seems like a good night for the abuelos to come," he says. Grandpa winks at me.

Ray starts to chase me. "Stop," I say. "Stop, stop!"

Ray stops. He doesn't move. "Shshsh," he whispers. "Listen. Someone's at the front door."

I jump up and run to my father. He walks toward the door, and Ray and I run to hide behind Mamá. We hold hands tight. Far away, I hear drumbeats.

"Ray, listen," I say. "Listen. Drums."

Our uncle comes in and says, "Buenas noches, buenas noches." My tío is wearing his funny shoes like he always does.

"Buenas noches, Tío," we say.

"They're coming," he says. "The abuelos are coming."

"Vamos, let's go," my parents say, helping us put on our coats.

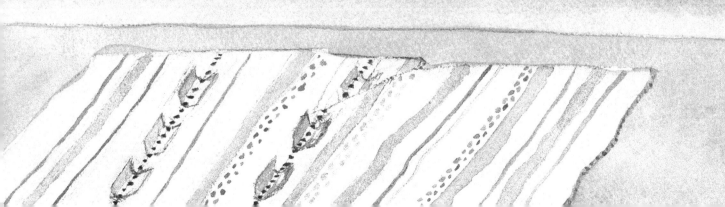

Outside, people are building a huge luminaria.
Our friends call us to run around the bonfire with
them.

"They're coming! The abuelos are coming!" the
older children yell.

We look up. They are coming — all hairy and
sooty!

"Ooooo, Ooooo, Ooooo," squeal the abuelos.
"Ooooo, Ooooo, Ooooo."

"Ooooo, Ooooo, Ooooo," the children of the
pueblo call back. "Ooooo."

Grandpa pats my head. Ray takes my hand,
and we start to run.

The abuelos stomp down from the mountain calling in high voices, "Who's been goo-ood? Who's been ba-ad? Naughty children make us ma-a-ad. Ooooo, Ooooo, Ooooo."

We run around the luminaria screaming and laughing. "Run, Amelia, run," shouts Ray. "Don't let the abuelos catch us."

I see an abuelo running out to grab us. "Run, Ray," I scream. "Run! Run!"

The abuelo gets closer and closer, squealing, "Ooooo." He grabs Ray's coat and won't let go. I look up at his sooty, hairy face, at his ragged clothes. "Have you been goo-oo-ood?" the abuelo asks Ray.

"Let him go!" I say, tugging on the abuelo's ragged coat. "You let my brother go!"

"You want me to let your brother go?" the abuelo asks me.

"Yes, yes," I say. "Let my brother go! I see something fall near the abuelo's shoes.

"Give me my mask!" growls the abuelo.

"Run, Ray, run," I yell.

I grab the mask and try to run away. The abuelo covers his face with one hand. He grabs my coat with the other. I pull and pull to get away. When I look down, I see his funny shoes.

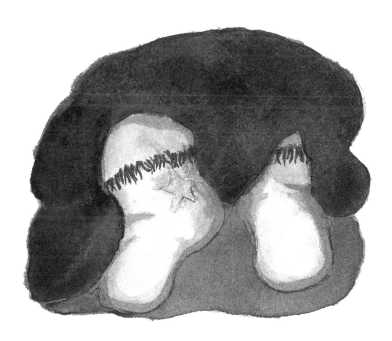

Everyone is running and shouting around us. Someone
bumps into me, and I drop the mask. The abuelo quickly
grabs it. Before he can put his mask back on, I look up.
My uncle! He winks and puts his finger on his lips. I pull
my coat hard and run away, but Tío chases me. I hear my
friends call, "Run, Amelia, run!"

Some of the big boys shout, "Jingle bells. Abuelo
smells." Papá grabs my hand and runs with me. Ray and
Grandpa run beside us.

"Ooooo," the abuelos call, laughing and chasing us all
around the luminaria. I feel safe holding Papá's hand,
and I start to laugh, too.

"Ooooo," we all call back as we race around the
crackling bonfire.

Our aunt opens her front door, and we all rush inside. It smells like warm sugar. Tía and her friends have baked homemade bizcochitos, our favorite little anise cookies, and Mamá has brought her empanadas.

The abuelo with the funny shoes comes toward us. He pulls Ray and me to the center of the room. In a high voice, the abuelo asks us to dance. He whines, "Bai-ai-ai-len, bai-ai-len." In his funny voice he sings, "Turún, tun, tun. Turún, tun, tun."

Ray and I dance. Everyone claps. Another abuelo starts to play a fiddle. Then suddenly everyone is dancing. The abuelo with the funny shoes dances with my aunt, and he dances with Mamá. Then he takes off his mask, and my uncle dances with Ray and me.

Author's Note

I BEGAN spending time in Santa Fe, New Mexico, where I now live, in 1994. Since I'm interested in cultural traditions, I visited museums and read about the customs of northern New Mexico. The tradition of "los abuelos" intrigued me. Luckily, it intrigued my publisher Patsy Aldana, too.

"Los abuelos" meant "the grandfathers" to me until I began reading references to the unique winter tradition of "los abuelos," popular in New Mexican villages in the past. I'm grateful to the scholars who study and write about such traditions and to the artists and community activists who instruct us and even re-create these customs from long ago.

On a visit to the Millicent Rogers Museum in Taos, I purchased the booklet, "Oremos, Oremos: Midwinter Masquerades," which explains, primarily through interviews, the tradition of sooty mountain men who appeared with frightening masks to check on the behavior of children. I'd seen a photo of a re-enactment, showing the excitement and anticipation, the bonfires created by the community, the villagers dressed as scary "abuelos" in the world-wide custom of cautionary tales — in this case, the bogeymen (and sometimes women and older children) reinforcing to the younger ones, through a bit of fear and fun, the importance of learning their prayers and minding their parents.

The scariness and laughter reminded me of Halloween, but "los abuelos" had a strong family and community theme, evidenced by the multi-generational closing fiesta.

Life is full of surprises. When my husband, a professor of anthropology, visited Japan last year, he saw a re-enactment of the "Namahage," a similar tradition of masked men who made surprise visits to make sure children had been studying.

Since I'm easily frightened, I chose to write a gentle version of how I imagine a spunky little girl responding to a visit by "los abuelos." Enjoy!

Pat Mora

CPSIA information can be obtained
at www.ICGtesting.com
Printed in the USA
JSHW051205201121
20642JS00007B/16